For my father, Robbie Jennings, who works
for peace – *PG*

For Leah, Ellis & Jodie – *CP*

BLOOMSBURY
CHILDREN'S
BOOKS

Published by Bloomsbury, New York and London
Distributed to the trade by Holtzbrinck Publishers

Library of Congress Cataloging in Publication Data:
Goodhart, Pippa.
Arthur's Tractor / by Pippa Goodhart; illustrated by Colin Paine. p. cm.
Summary: Unaware that a princess in distress and a dragon on the loose are right
behind him, Arthur the farmer thinks that the strange noises he keeps hearing are
being made by his tractor breaking down.
ISBN 1-58234-847-2 (alk. paper)
[1. Farmers--Fiction. 2. Tractors--Fiction. 3. Princesses--Fiction. 4. Dragons--
Fiction. 5. Humorous Stories.] I. Paine, Colin, ill. II. Title.
PZ7.G6125 Ar 2003
[E]—dc21
2002028030

First U.S. Edition 2003
Printed in Singapore by Tien Wah Press
3 5 7 9 10 8 6 4 2

Bloomsbury USA Children's Books
175 Fifth Avenue
New York, NY 10010

Arthur's Tractor

a fairy tale with mechanical parts

by Pippa Goodhart

illustrated by
Colin Paine

BLOOMSBURY
CHILDREN'S
BOOKS

Arthur's tractor plowed up and down, turning green to brown.

Chugga thrum, chugga thrum, chugga chugga thrum.
Chugga thrum, chugga thrum, chugga chugga –

EEEK!

Arthur stamped down the brake and stopped the tractor.
"Well, knobble my kneecaps, whatever can that EEEK be?"

Arthur turned off the engine and got down from his cab. He stood for a while and scratched his head. Then he said, "That must be the sprocket spring sprigget needing a twist and an oil."

So Arthur twisted and oiled.

He started up his tractor, and now there was no EEEK, just...

Chugga thrum, chugga thrum,

chugga chugga thrum.

"Good," said Arthur.

"Well, bless my blisters, whatever can that THUD THUD THUD be?" Arthur turned off the engine and got down from his cab. He stood for a while and scratched his head. Then he said,

THUD THUD THUD!

"That must be the old bundle weaver running loose."
So he gave the bundle weaver a kick, and when he started up
his tractor there was no THUD THUD THUD, just...

Chugga thrum, chugga thrum, chugga chugga thrum.

"Good," said Arthur. Then . . .

Chugga thrum, chugga thrum, chugga chugga –

CRASH!

"Well, top and tail a turnip, whatever can that CRASH be?" Arthur turned off the engine and got down from his cab. He stood for a while and he scratched his head. Then he said, "That must have been the curling blade hitting a stone. That will have to be sheared and shuffled and sharpened now."

So Arthur took out his tools.

He sheared.

He shuffled.

He began to sharpen…
but something jogged his arm
and the curling blade shattered.

"Oh, dollops of dung, the blim blam blade has broken!"

"Here," said Arthur.
"May I have that old sword?"

"And if you could blow there,
that would help."

"May I have a bit of that to wipe the blade clean?"

"And if you'd hold that in place that would help."

Arthur and his new friend Edith hemmed and jiggered and fixed a fine, sharp, new curling blade.

The blade was fixed, but the lady lingered.

"That's a finely tuned and turned-out tractor you've got there," she said.

"It is," said Arthur. "But, if I may say so, Edith, you're rather well tuned and turned out yourself."

"Oh!" said Lady Edith. "And you, Arthur, are as handsome as a well-polished tractor."

"Nobody's ever said anything like that to me before," said Arthur.

Arthur took off his cap and he scratched his head
and he thought for a while. Then he said,
"Would you care to share this tractor with me, Edith?
And the soil too? We could sow and reap together and
forever. What do you say?"

"I think that would be good," said Lady Edith. "Now
pass me that can and I'll oil that coil bolt brandisher
before the dang thing bangles free."

And they all lived happily ever after.